INVEST KIDS™

CASH AND ATMs

Gillian Houghton

PowerKiDS
press™

New York

JUN 3 0 2009

Published in 2009 by The Rosen Publishing Group, Inc.
29 East 21st Street, New York, NY 10010

First Edition

Editor: Joanne Randolph
Book Design: Julio Gil
Photo Researcher: Jessica Gerweck

Photo Credits: Cover, p. 5 © Andersen Ross/Getty Images; back cover, pp. 6, 9 (inset), 14, 17, 21 Shutterstock.com; p. 9 (main) © Getty Images; p. 10 © National Geographic/Getty Images; p. 13 © Nicholas Prior/Getty Images; p. 18 © DreamPictures/Getty Images.

Library of Congress Cataloging-in-Publication Data

Houghton, Gillian.
  Cash and ATMs / Gillian Houghton. — 1st ed.
      p. cm. — (Invest kids)
  Includes index.
  ISBN 978-1-4358-2771-4 (library binding) — ISBN 978-1-4358-3206-0 (pbk.)
ISBN 978-1-4358-3212-1 (6-pack)
  1. Money—Juvenile literature. 2. Automated tellers—Juvenile literature. I. Title.
  HG221.5.H68 2009
  332.4—dc22
                                        2008035165

Manufactured in the United States of America

Contents

Talking Cash   4
What Is Cash?   7
A Short History of Money   8
Bank on It!   11
Add It Up!   12
What Is an ATM?   15
How Do ATMs Work?   16
Using an ATM   19
Stay Safe!   20
Be Careful with Your Cash   22
Glossary   23
Index   24
Web Sites   24

Talking Cash

Picture yourself as a **customer** in line at a store. We go to stores to buy the things we need and want. You need to buy some food to eat. "That's 4 dollars for the box of crackers, 3 dollars for the jug of milk, and 75 cents for the bananas. That will be 7 dollars and 75 cents, please," says the man at the **cash register**.

You count your money and hand it to the man. He counts it again and puts it in the register. If you give him more money than you owe, he gives you change. You put your food in a bag and are on your way. You just used cash!

We can use cash to buy food at the store, as this family is doing.
Cash lets us buy the things we need to live healthy lives.

This picture shows a 10-dollar bill, a 20-dollar bill, and some coins. We use bills and coins to pay for goods and services.

What Is Cash?

Cash is money in the form of metal coins and paper bills. Different countries or groups of countries have different currencies, or kinds of cash. In the United States, we use dollars and cents. Our dollars come in different denominations, or amounts of money. There are bills worth, or equal to, 1, 2, 5, 10, 20, 50, and 100 dollars.

The penny is the smallest denomination of coin in the United States. It is worth 1 cent. It takes 100 cents to equal 1 dollar. A nickel is worth 5 cents. A dime is worth 10 cents. A quarter is worth 25 cents. There are also coins worth 1 dollar.

A Short History of Money

    A very long time ago, people did not use money. They hunted and gathered, or went out and found, food and the things they needed to live. About 10,000 years ago, people started planting crops and living in villages. They traded for the things they needed.

    Around 2500 BC, people in present-day Iraq began to **exchange** balls of gold and silver for goods. About 1,900 years later, the people of present-day Turkey made the first flat coins **stamped** with a special mark. The first paper money was printed in China in AD 812 and spread to Europe in the 1300s.

This is a market from the 1400s, where people came to trade for goods.
Inset: This Roman coin was likely used over 1,600 years ago.

This person is working in the national mint. Every day, the government stamps 4 million quarters, 10 million dimes, 2 million nickels, and 25 million pennies!

Bank on It!

In 1863, the United States made a **national** banking **system**. This meant that a national **mint** would make all the money. It also meant that this money would be backed by the government's supply of gold. This system was called the gold standard. A standard is something against which other things are measured.

Until the 1970s, you could take your paper money to the government and exchange it for its **value** in gold. This changed in 1971. Today, bills and coins have no value other than the value we as a country agree that they have.

Add It Up!

Remember our trip to the store? When we handed our money to the man behind the counter, we agreed that crackers, milk, and bananas had a certain value. We owed 7 dollars and 75 cents. We write that amount as $7.75.

There are many **combinations** of bills and cents that add up to this amount. We could have handed the man one 5-dollar bill, two 1-dollar bills, seven dimes, and one nickel. We could have paid using 775 pennies or 31 quarters! Can you think of another combination of bills and coins that add up to $7.75?

This boy is counting up his savings. You may start off with just change in your piggy bank, but as you save more, those coins will add up to dollars.

These people are using ATMs. People visit ATMs when they need cash to buy things, such as food, clothing, or a train ticket.

What Is an ATM?

When you open an **account** at a bank, you are given a small plastic card. There is a magnetic strip or a microchip on one side, and on the other side, your name and account number are printed. This piece of plastic, which might be called an ATM card or a debit card, lets you use a machine called an ATM to **withdraw** and **deposit** cash.

"ATM" stands for "automated teller machine." These machines can be found in banks, in stores, and on the sidewalk. They allow bank customers to withdraw and deposit money at any time.

How Do ATMs Work?

An ATM is a kind of computer. It is connected to the bank's computer. When you withdraw money from an ATM, it asks the bank's computer if you have enough money in your account to do so.

There are four main parts of an ATM bank customers should know. The card reader is the slot where you put your ATM card. The keypad is made up of small buttons with numbers on them. The display screen asks you questions and gives facts about your account in writing. The cash dispenser counts the bills and dispenses, or passes, them to you.

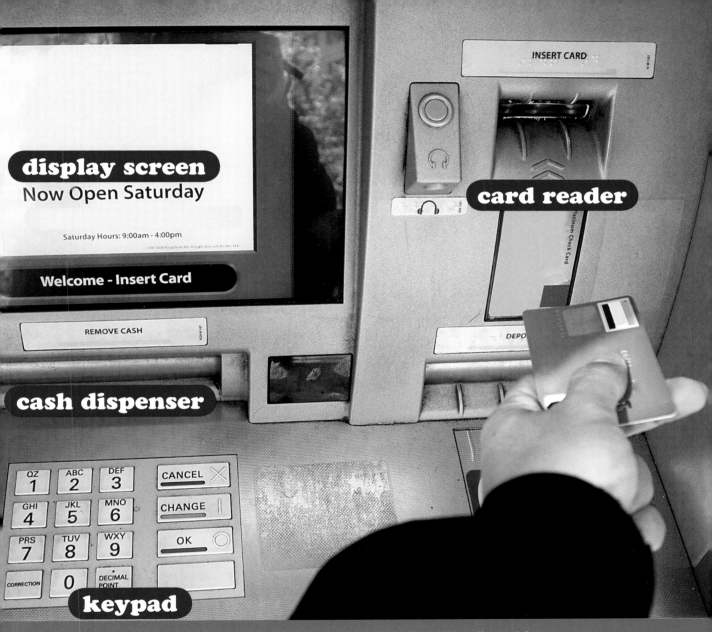

display screen

Now Open Saturday

Saturday Hours: 9:00am - 4:00pm

Welcome - Insert Card

REMOVE CASH

cash dispenser

card reader

INSERT CARD

DEPO

Platinum Check Card

QZ 1 | ABC 2 | DEF 3 | CANCEL ✕
GHI 4 | JKL 5 | MNO 6 | CHANGE |
PRS 7 | TUV 8 | WXY 9 | OK ○
CORRECTION | 0 | DECIMAL POINT |

keypad

This picture shows the main parts of an ATM. The first thing you do when you visit an ATM is put your card in the card reader.

Using an ATM is a quick, easy way to do your banking. ATMs can be found in malls, on street corners, or in banks, and they let a person take out or deposit cash anytime.

Using an ATM

When someone is ready to use an ATM, she pushes the card into the card reader. The display screen will ask for a PIN, or **personal identification number**. It is usually four secret numbers that bank customers choose to keep their accounts safe. The person types in the numbers using the keypad.

Then the display screen will ask what she would like to do. To take out cash, the person presses the button to make a withdrawal. Then she enters the amount of money needed. The ATM will pass the money through the cash dispenser.

Stay Safe!

ATMs ask you for a PIN before they let you withdraw or deposit money. Pick one that is easy for you to remember. Do not share your PIN with anyone, and do not write it down. This way, no one can use your ATM card except you.

People who use ATMs could get robbed since they are taking out cash. Keep an eye on the people around you when you use an ATM, and put your cash out of sight quickly.

Many ATMs have cameras that record what happens around the machine. These might scare some robbers away but not all of them.

When using an ATM, stand right in front of the screen. This makes it hard for people to see what you are typing on the keypad or to take your money from the cash dispenser.

Be Careful with Your Cash

We spend money on things we need and on things we just want. We need food, a place to live, and some clothes to wear. We want all sorts of things, such as toys or a new bike. We need to make smart decisions about how we spend our cash.

When you walk up to a cash register, ask yourself if you are buying something you need or want. Before you buy things you want, be sure you save money for things you need. Better yet, instead of spending your money, you can put it in a savings account. A bank will pay you money every month, so your cash can grow!

GLOSSARY

account (UH-kownt) A special place where a bank keeps money set aside for a person.

cash register (KASH REH-juh-ster) A machine that adds up how much things cost and stores money.

combinations (kahm-buh-NAY-shunz) Things that are mixed or brought together.

customer (KUS-tuh-mur) A person who buys goods or services.

deposit (dih-PAH-zut) To put something in.

exchange (iks-CHAYNJ) To give one thing and get a different thing in return.

mint (MINT) A place where a country's official money is made.

national (NASH-nul) Belonging to the country.

personal identification number (PERS-nul eye-den-tuh-fih-KAY-shun NUM-ber) A number a bank customer uses to be able to withdraw or deposit money from his or her account at an ATM.

system (SIS-tem) A way of doing something.

value (VAL-yoo) An amount that people agree something is worth.

withdraw (with-DRAW) To take something out.

INDEX

A
account, 15–16, 19, 22
amount(s), 7, 12, 19

B
bills, 7, 11–12, 16

C
cash register, 4, 22
cents, 4, 7, 12
change, 4
coins, 7–8, 11–12
countries, 7, 11
currencies, 7
customer(s), 4, 15–16, 19

D
denominations, 7
dollars, 4, 7, 12

F
form, 7

G
groups, 7

J
jug, 4

M
mint, 11

P
penny, 7, 12
people, 8, 19–20
piece, 15
plastic, 15

S
store(s), 4, 12, 15
system, 11

U
United States, 7, 11

V
value, 11–12

WEB SITES

Due to the changing nature of Internet links, PowerKids Press has developed an online list of Web sites related to the subject of this book. This site is updated regularly. Please use this link to access the list:
www.powerkidslinks.com/ikids/cash/